# Jaden Toussaint, The Greatest

## The Greatest

Episode 5:

## MISSION STAR-POWER

Written by Marti Dumas

Illustrated by Stephanie Parcus

## Plum Street Press

A Division of Yes, MAM Creations

Published by **Plum Street Press**
Copyright © 2017 by **Marti Dumas**

ISBN: 978-1-943169-27-6

# Contents

# Prologue

SPEAKS KINDNESS, OOZES CONFIDENCE.

JADEN TOUSSAINT

Specializes in: Knowing Stuff. And also, ninja dancing. He's really, really good at ninja dancing.

## OWEN

Jokester and action expert.

Extreme dinosaur safari bungee jumping? Owen is your guy.

## THE FRIENDS

## EVIE

Don't let the cuteness fool you.

This girl packs a punch. Excels at: Being in Charge.

SONJA

Cicada hunter and math whiz.

Also draws
excellent rainbows.

WINSTON

Can quote stats
from every World
Cup final.*

*that he has been alive for

Spots hurt feelings and distracted goalies from miles away.

Past president, International Society of Stealthy Felines. Resigned in scandal. Likes to be held like a baby and scratch stuff.

GRANDMASTER, CAT CHESS.

GRIS GRIS

# ANIMAL OF MYSTERY

Guinea Pig never has the same name
two weeks in a row.

This week, you may call him His Imperial
Majesty, King of the Forest. (Maj for short.)

**Baba:**

Tall. Competitive. Competitive about being tall. Gives great piggyback rides. Prefers to be called "baba," which means "father" in Swahili. Does not speak Swahili.

**Mama:**

Loving. No nonsense. Most often seen reading fantasy books or experimenting with bean desserts. Gives good hugs.

**Sissy:**

Reader. Writer. Animal lover. Once gave up meat for 6 months, but was broken by the smell of turkey bacon. Plans to be the first PhD chemist to star in a Broadway musical.

# Chapter 1
## A Star is Born

On poster:
HOW TO BE A SCIENTIST
ASK A QUESTION
DO BACKGROUND RESEARCH
MAKE A HYPOTHESIS
TEST YOUR HYPOTHESIS BY DOING AN EXPERIMENT
ANALYZE YOUR DATA AND DRAW A CONCLUSION
COMMUNICATE YOUR RESULTS
REPEAT!

*Jaden Toussaint loved to read.*

He especially loved to read on Sissy's new e-reader.

They "read" outside.

They "read" in the car.

They even "read" in Sissy's top bunk.

They may have, occasionally, used Sissy's e-reader for stuff besides reading, but that had only happened once or twice. Maybe three times.

Okay. Maybe it was more than three. Seven. Eight, max.

But however many times it was, for some reason, Mama was not happy about it when she found out.

Luckily for Sissy, she had JT on her side.

SELECT PLAYER MODE

ANIMAL EXPERT

BABY BROTHER

BUCKET-FILLER

FRIEND

GREAT DEBATER

NEGOTIATOR

NINJA DANCER

PROBLEM-SOLVER

READER

SCIENTIST

TEAM LEADER

TEAM PLAYER

THESPIAN

THINKER

WRITER

Thanks to JT, after several rounds of negotiation, Sissy got off with a warning.

She could keep her e-reader as long as she promised to use it only for
1. reading books
and
2. making stuff.

REQUESTS
~~DEMANDS~~

- Use the e-reader when you say it's ok. ~~any time we want~~

- ~~All the Halloween~~ we don't really need this ~~candy~~

- ~~$1,000,000~~ Please?

Jaden Toussaint was a tiny bit disappointed to have to delete all the games.

Smoothie Samurai and Vet Shoppe #187 were a lot of fun. And they taught you useful information like apple seeds being a tiny bit poisonous and that baby dragons don't care for peanut butter. But Jaden Toussaint wasn't disappointed for long, because the very next time Sissy was allowed to use her e-reader, she said five magic words:

*Want    to    make    a    video?*

# Chapter 2

## TUBERS IN PROGRESS

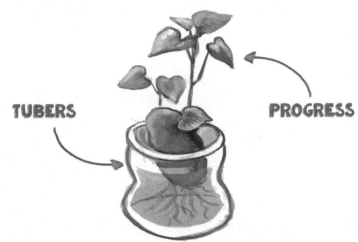

TUBERS          PROGRESS

WARNING: LEAVES NOT EDIBLE FOR GUINEA PIGS OF ANY NAME.

It took a minute for the magic of Sissy's words to sink in. Jaden Toussaint had never made a video before. He had watched lots of videos, though, mostly of the Animal Guys, mostly on TubeTube.

In the Animal Guys' TubeTube videos, they were always someplace cool like the Serengeti or the Amazon rainforest.

Mama would never let JT and Sissy go all the way to the Amazon rainforest. At least not on a school night.

If only we had a time machine... No! A teleporter!

JT felt a little unsure about becoming a TubeTuber, but he decided to give it a try. Sissy was right a lot of the time. Not as often as he was, but those were still good odds.

**HEIGHT CHART**

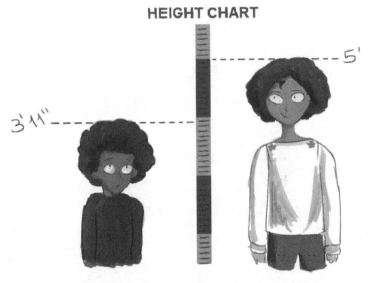

3' 11"

5'

**RIGHTNESS CHART**

ALMOST ALWAYS RIGHT

MOSTLY RIGHT

*RIGHTNESS APPROXIMATE. FIGURES MAY NOT BE TO SCALE.

That turned out to be an excellent decision because, as it turned out, Jaden Toussaint and Sissy were excellent at making videos.

*They made comedies.*

*They made tragedies. Sort of.*

*They even made information videos.*

Jaden Toussaint liked the information videos the best. He was surprised to learn that being super-smart about animal facts on camera was kind of his thing. In fact, JT was so good at it that he and Sissy even made special graphics and recorded music to use for an intro. It wasn't quite as good as the Animal Guys, but it was pretty close.

He couldn't wait to show Mama and Baba so they could upload the video and he could get 1 billion likes and become an overnight success by the time he went to school the next day.

His friends would be so impressed.

**Problem:** Mama and Baba said *no*.

They said no the first time, the 17th time, and all the times in between. They kept saying something about the problem being lots of people seeing it, and he kept trying to explain that lots of people seeing it was exactly the point. Unfortunately, no matter how much he tried to help them, they just couldn't seem to understand that part.

"How about we invite your friends over for a movie night?" Mama asked. "You can show them your video, and they can show you they 'like' it. I bet Grandfather would come."

*"I know,"* JT said, frowning.

Pause.

He didn't really know. I mean,
he knew that Grandfather would
come if he did something cool.
Grandfather always came when he
did something cool. But that wasn't
what he was talking about and "*I
know*" was the first thing he thought
of to say. He didn't mean to be
rude, but how was he supposed to
become an internationally famous
tv animal scientist if the only people
who saw him were his friends and
family?

Unpause.

It was time to make a plan.

# Chapter 3
## ARTS CELEBRATION

JT was working on a plan when he got to circle time the next day.

His best plan at that point involved accidentally going viral when someone discovered him tap dancing with live penguins.  If anyone saw him doing something that cool, they would definitely record it and post it on the internet. And a video like that would get tons of likes.

There were penguins at the aquarium. He was sure the zoo keepers would let him go behind the scenes once they realized how much he knew about animals.

The part he wasn't sure about was how long it would take the penguins to learn the dance steps. So that plan still needed some work.

He tried to pay attention when Ms. Bates started talking. Ms. Bates usually had important things for them to discuss.

"Readers, writers, thinkers, and artists, it's almost time for the Arts Celebration."

Everybody cheered. The Arts Celebration was enough to put his plan on pause. It was like a fair, but better. Every kid got to run around and buy snacks with their friends, but also be a famous artist at the same time. People would stop you and ask to take your picture next to your art. Sometimes they even asked for your autograph.

JT had never gotten to be a part of the Arts Celebration before. None of the kindergartners had. But he had seen Sissy do it and he couldn't wait for his turn.

Ms. Bates waited for all the cheering to quiet down before she continued. "We just have to decide what kind of performance we want to do. The third graders are dancing. The fourth graders are juggling and tumbling. The fifth graders are singing songs they learned at Camp Planet Earth. What do you think we should do?"

...PURPLE AND ORANGE AND BLUE...

Everyone had lots of ideas.

...AND THAT'S JUST WHAT THEY'LL DO...

Evie suggested they sing a Nancy Sinatra song that she claimed had been especially written about her boots. Sonja agreed about singing, but she thought they should sing a rainbow.

Winston suggested they do sand art meditation. Owen said something about jutsu.

Ms. Bates was just about to get everyone settled down again, when...

Jaden Toussaint's hand shot up into the air. "Ms. Bates?" he said. It took a second for her to respond. Owen had gotten pretty riled up with his jutsus. "How about we make a play? Theater's an art we can celebrate, right?  And if we make our own play we can use everybody's ideas."

"Theater is definitely an art we can celebrate. That's a great idea! What does everyone think about that?"

They all cheered again, Jaden Toussaint the loudest of all. Not only did doing a play at the Arts Celebration sound like a lot of fun, but it also solved his other problem. This would be way better for getting famous than dancing penguins. The school had its own TubeTube channel. They posted videos of all the school performances there, including the ones from the Arts Celebration. Why hadn't he thought of that before?

All he had to do was write the most awesome play ever, be the star, learn all his lines, learn everybody else's lines in case they forgot them, and be extra entertaining so their video would get one million likes like the cats who keep diaries. Easy. This was going to be S-WEET!

# Chapter 4

## STAGE FRIGHT

Jaden Toussaint and his friends were so excited about the play that they talked about it all the way through recess.

"We should definitely have a goddess," Evie said.

"Ooh! Does that mean we can have a rainbow bridge?" Sonja asked.

"That's a good idea!" Owen added. "I'll be the god of jutsu."

JT loved the idea. Even the 5th graders passing by thought it sounded cool.

The only problem was Jaden Toussaint was too busy dancing and thinking about his upcoming fame to notice that Winston was not saying anything. In fact, JT didn't realize anything was wrong until the class started working on the play after recess.

Evie and Sonja had just told Ms. Bates their idea of doing a play about gods and goddesses with a rainbow bridge. The class decided that Sonja would be Freya of Asgard, Evie would be mischievous Loki (as long as she could still sing the song about her boots), and Jaden Toussaint would be Zeus. He couldn't remember if it was Zeus or Thor who had the rainbow bridge, but he decided on Zeus because Zeus had a better costume.
No one seemed to mind.

He was just trying to decide which sheet of his would make the most awesome toga, when he noticed Winston sitting off by himself. Winston wasn't giggling and laughing like everyone else. He just looked...kind of...sad.

At first Jaden Toussaint thought that Winston might be meditating. He did that sometimes. But when everyone went off to start making their costumes, Winston just stayed in the same place. Something didn't seem right. JT thought he would check in just in case.

"What's wrong, Winston?" JT asked.

"I'm just thinking about a lotus flower," Winston said.

"Is that the god you're going to be in the play?" JT had never heard of a flower god before, but Lotus was as good a name for one as any.

"Oh. I'm not going to be in the play."

"What? Why not?" Jaden Toussaint could barely get the words out.

"I don't want to," Winston said simply.

"But I do want to help Sonja make that rainbow bridge. That sounds like fun. Want to come?"

JT just stood still. He was thinking about what Winston had said. It didn't make any sense. Why on earth would he not want to be in the play? It was all well and fine to help with the sets, but if Winston didn't come on the stage during their performance, he wouldn't be in the video. And if Winston wasn't in the video, he wouldn't become internet famous with them. And if Winston didn't become internet famous with them, he wouldn't be invited to go on tour with them in the stage version of *Animal Guys, Animal Guys Live!*, JT had been planning in his mind. And if Winston didn't tour with them in *Animal Guys Live!*, they might lose touch and stop being friends.

Did Winston not want to be their friend anymore? It was all too much to handle.

Owen saw the horrified look on Jaden Toussaint's face. "What happened to you?" he asked. "Was it aliens?"

JT shook his head. "Winston doesn't want to be in the play. I think he might not want to be our friend anymore."

"Hunh." Owen shrugged, looking over at Winston. "I think he still wants to be my friend."

"That's not helping, Owen," Evie said.

Then she turned to JT. "Of course Winston still wants to be your friend. He wants to be all our friend. That's not the problem at all. The problem is that Winston has...

stage fright."

Jaden Toussaint gasped. Owen gasped, too, but then he said, "Wait. How do you know Winston has stage fright?"

Evie pointed at Winston. "Do you see the way he's shaking?"

JT and Owen both nodded.

"He's quaking with fear. My cousin had stage fright once and that's definitely one of the symptoms."

The way Winston was shaking could have been from fear, but it also could have been that he and Sonja were giggling a lot. It was hard to tell. He had his back turned.

"And do you see how he's swaying?" JT and Owen nodded again. It might have been wiggly dancing, but Winston was definitely moving around. "Dizziness. Classic stage fright."

Just then, Winston raised his hand. "Ms. Bates? May I go get some water, please?"

"Oh, no!" Evie said. "Dry mouth. Y'all, that's another symptom of stage fright."

"But he's smiling," Owen said.

"That's not a smile, it's a facial tic."

"See how he keeps doing it over and over again? That only happens when stage fright is really, really, bad. He's worse off than I thought. We have to do something."

Stage fright sounded horrible.

"We have to help him," Jaden Toussaint said. "Get Sonja. I know what to do."

# Chapter 5
## ACTION!

Jaden Toussaint, Evie, Sonja, and Owen got special permission from Ms. Bates to go to the library. Sonja thought they were there to do research on their parts for the play.

"I already know a lot about Freya of Asgard," Sonja said. "She has a magic necklace, her chariot is pulled by two cats, she--"

"That's not why we came to the library, Sonja," Evie said.

"It's not?" Sonja asked.

"No," JT said, trying to keep his voice quiet. They were in the library after all. "We're here because we think Winston has... [dunh Dunh DUNH] stage fright."

Sonja gasped. "No wonder he was giggling so much! I giggle when I'm nervous, too. That explains why he doesn't want a part in our play. What should we do?"

"We're scientists, right?" Jaden Toussaint said. "First stop: research."

Jaden Toussaint and his friends sprang into action. Ms. Barbier, the librarian, was there to help.
It turned out that Evie was right. People with stage fright really did feel sick. Having a fluttering heart, shaky legs, and sweating hands sounded awful. Jaden Toussaint felt terrible for Winston. Luckily, there were lots of suggestions to help cure him. There might actually have been too many.

By the time they finished their research, they had filled a few pages (front and back) with possible cures.

"How do we know which one will work?" Sonja asked.

"We'll just have to test them all," Jaden Toussaint said.

And that's exactly what they did. The hardest part turned out to be convincing Winston that he had stage fright in the first place.

"How would you feel standing on stage in front of a thousand million people?" Owen began.

"You mean a billion?" Winston asked. "I might feel a little nervous."

"I knew it!" Owen said. "Classic stage fright."

"And do you or do you not want to have a part in the play?" Evie asked.

"No," Winston said. "I don't want a part. Not really."

"Ooh," Evie said, concerned. "Sounds like stage fright."

"Well," JT asked, "do you want to be extra, super famous and travel the world performing 'Animal Guys Live and on Stage!' with us?"

Winston thought about it for a moment. "I don't think so..." he said.

"See!" They all said at once. "Stage fright!"

"And all this time I thought it just wasn't my thing. Maybe I really do have stage fright. What do I do?"

JT presented Winston their research,

then they all got down to work.

For the next few days, they did everything they could to help Winston with his stage fright. Winston didn't have a part to learn, so he used JT's part instead. At first he read the lines nervously.

JT observed and took careful notes. Then they started the experiments.

*They tried deep breathing.*

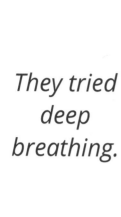

*They tried orange juice.*

They tried hopping on one foot, having him tickle the roof of his mouth with his tongue, and counting to 10 at the same time.

They even tried the trickiest one of all:

having Winston personally meet
and become best friends with every
single member of the audience.

Pause.

They weren't really sure who would be in the audience, and it was possible that they didn't actually give Winston enough time to become *best* friends with everyone, but they figured if he said hi to all the kindergartners, squirrels, and cicadas on the playground, that would be close enough.

Unpause.

Winston's performance really seemed to have improved.

But whenever they asked him how he felt about being in the play, Winston always had the same answer: "It still doesn't really feel like my thing."

"It's hopeless!" Evie said.

"We didn't cure him," Owen said sadly.

"The dress rehearsal is today and Winston still doesn't want a part," Sonja exclaimed.

"Don't blame yourselves, guys," Winston said. "You tried really hard."

"We're not done, yet." JT declared. "There's only one way to know for sure. Winston, would you be willing to do my part at the dress rehearsal this afternoon?"

"I guess so," Winston said.

It was settled. Ms. Bates was a little confused about why Winston would be performing Jaden Toussaint's part at the dress rehearsal. She kept saying something about the dress rehearsal being for the people who are actually going to perform.

JT couldn't see what the problem was. He knew his part perfectly and this was their last chance to get Winston to overcome his stage fright so he could join them in the play. Sonja was all ready for him to play one of the cats who pulled her chariot if he changed his mind.

In the end, Ms. Bates agreed that they could practice the play twice: once with Winston and once with JT.

Everything went according to plan. Winston did JT's part, and when Ms. Bates paused for JT and Winston to trade places, Sonja, Evie, and Owen crowded around, too, to see how Winston felt.

"It's still not my thing," Winston began, "but..."

"I don't mind it that much. I could be the cat, I guess."

Winston smiled and JT, Owen, Evie, and Sonja all cheered.

"I'm so happy to see everyone so happy," Ms. Bates said, "but I'm afraid we need to get the real dress rehearsal done before we run out of time. The performance is tonight and it's almost the 4th grade's turn to practice."

Ms. Bates was right. The fourth graders were beginning to line up in the auditorium. JT felt a tiny little flutter in his stomach, but pushed it aside. It was probably just gas.

Jaden Toussaint took his place at the center of the stage. His mouth felt a little dry. They'd taken so much extra time for Winston that JT didn't want to waste more time asking for the water fountain. He'd wait until they were done.

Then, right before Ms. Bates shouted, "Action!" the unthinkable happened:

The principal, Ms. Nelson, walked into the auditorium.

Now, Ms. Nelson was a nice principal. Really, she was. She gave hugs and stickers and always reminded everyone to be kind. But something about Ms. Nelson standing in the front row reminded Jaden Toussaint of all the other people who would be in the first row. And the second row. And the third row.

People he didn't know.
Looking at him.
Waiting for him to mess up.

JT's mouth got even drier. His legs began to shake. He thought his heart skipped a thousand beats. And when it was time for him to speak his mouth was so dry that none of the words would come out.

He could feel his star-power falling as he stood frozen in place. It was the worst possible thing.

Stage fright.

# Chapter 6
## STAR-CROSSED

I AM MIGHTY ZEUS, GOD OF THUNDER.

Winston stood next to JT and said his lines for him to finish the dress rehearsal. That was certainly kind of Winston, but Jaden Toussaint didn't feel any better. His life was ruined.

All he had ever wanted to be was a famous animal scientist who teaches kids stuff on tv.

Now the Animal Guys would never let him join their team or take over the show when they retired.

And what was the point in creating *Animal Guys Live!* if he was too scared to say anything on stage?

There was no job for people who just stood really still every time they were in front of an audience. Was there?

As the 4th graders piled onstage to practice their circus routine, Jaden Toussaint could feel the tears welling up behind his eyes until eventually they just spilled over.

Everyone crowded around to hug him.

"It's not so bad. You can still be a famous animal scientist," Sonja said. "I don't think they all go on Broadway and tv and stuff."

"I know," JT said.

Pause.

He didn't really know. At least, he hadn't thought about it yet. All the animal scientists he knew did stuff on tv, but it made sense that there might be one or two others who didn't. But he wasn't like those not-tv scientists. He wanted to be on tv. Now he couldn't. Thinking about not-tv scientists didn't make him feel better. It kind of made him feel worse.

Unpause.

"We still have all the stuff from Winston!" Owen exclaimed. "We can cure you!"

Jaden Toussaint brightened a teensy bit,

but it didn't last for long.

They had tried almost all the cures they used on Winston (Ms. Bates wouldn't let them go get any squirrels), and not one of them worked. Jaden Toussaint still shivered and broke into a cold sweat at just the thought of going back on stage.

He felt awful. It had worked for Winston. Why hadn't it worked for him?

"Winston, what am I doing wrong?"

"I didn't want to say this, but I think I maybe never had stage fright at all. I was a little nervous at first, but not as much as you are."

"So you did all that stuff for nothing?" JT asked.

"I didn't mind. I'm just sorry it's not working for you. I know how much you want to be in the play."

JT did want to be in the play. He really, really did. He was just about to say that they should do all the cures again, just in case they had done one wrong the first time, when the 5th graders came in, Sissy included.

Sissy took one look at Jaden Toussaint and knew something was wrong. She rushed over to help.

"What's wrong, Toots?" Sissy asked. Jaden Toussaint told her. She hugged him really tightly. "Did you know that some of the greatest performers have stage fright?"

"I know," he said.

Pause.

He didn't really know. He just didn't want to seem completely hopeless and "I know" was the first thing he thought of to say.

Unpause.

"I bet even the Animal Guys have stage fright sometimes. We just have to figure out a strategy to help you get through it. Have you tried breathing?" Jaden Toussaint nodded.

"Imagining friendly faces in the audience?"

"Yep."

"Hopping on one foot and tickling the roof of your mouth with your tongue while you count to ten?"

"Yep. I tried that, too."

Thanks to his gigantic brain, most ideas just popped right into JT's head without him trying. But this stage fright thing was a toughie. For stubborn problems like this one, there was one surefire way to kick his brain into top gear:

Turn the Page!

# 3 MINUTE

SUNSHINE

*Moonlight*

GOOD TIMES

THE BOOGIE

# DANCE PARTY

CIRCUS

GOD OF THUNDER

NEBULA

LOOK OUT!
I THINK IT'S... YES!

STAR POWER

Then, out of nowhere, it started. That swirly, whirly, zinging feeling he got whenever he was on the verge of a brilliant idea. And just like that, Jaden Toussaint knew what to do.

# Chapter 7
## MAKE WAY FOR THESPIANS

At the performance that night, Sissy brought her e-reader and sat right in the front row. Mama and Baba were there, and so was Grandfather, but JT focused all his attention on Sissy. He was never nervous when he and Sissy made videos together, so he had the idea that if he tricked himself into thinking that it was just the two of them making a video, he might relax enough to perform.

And do you know what? That did the trick.
Concentrating on Sissy made it easy to
relax and get into character. He was so
relaxed that by the time he had to say his
lines, he had completely forgotten that he
wasn't Zeus in real life.

His words rolled like thunder and his
lightning bolts were feared by all. He still
felt nervous, but it gave him just enough
energy to do a great job.

Winston decided not to be in the play after all. He wasn't frightened. It just wasn't his thing. Ms. Bates put his name in the program as set designer, and he joined them on stage to take a bow. Then everyone went out to celebrate the Arts Celebration by eating beignets. Jaden Toussaint was just about to take a big, sugary bite, when Baba said something unexpected.

"Bruh, I know how much you want to get likes on your video. The school's TubeTube channel is private, so only school families can see the video from your performance. But y'all did such a good job that, if the other parents agree, Mama and I will try to get special permission to make it public. Just this once. You might even get a million likes," Baba said with a wink.

Jaden Toussaint thought about it, then he shook his head. "Nah," he said. "Maybe next year." He still wanted to be famous, but there was no rush.

# Gris-Gris' Cat Chess TubeTube Channel

Introduction to Cat Chess      1,002,892 likes

## Subscribe for more!

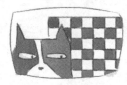     Mastering Cat Chess openings

Recommended Cat Chess Books

     Endgame fundamentals

# Epilogue

## THINGS TO DO BEFORE I AM A FAMOUS ANIMAL SCIENTIST

☑ 1. Eat ~~all~~ *as many* the Beignets as is humanly possible

⚠ Side effects:
- happiness
- tummy aches
- powdered sugar face/powdered sugar shirt/ powdered sugar hair

☐ 2. Build a time machine and/or teleportation device

⚠ Side effects
- makes it easier to get beignets
- possible time paradox and the undoing of the space-time continuum.

☐ 3. Learn to teach penguin choreography (JUST IN CASE)

⚠ Side effects
- Going viral (no vaccine required)
- Organic likes best (Do some likes have pesticides?)

BE KIND, BE RESPONSIBLE, DO YOUR BEST WORK

# WHO MADE

## About the Illustrator

Stephanie Parcus loves to create beautiful things. She grew up in Brazil, living off cartoons and bananas, then moved to Italy when she was 10, where she discovered Anime and Manga. Her dream of being a Pokémon trainer and her love for her dog, Fly, led her to become a veterinarian! When she's not on her farm retreat in Italy, she is traveling the world with the human who stole her heart.

# THIS BOOK? ...........................

## About the Author

Marti Dumas is a mama who spends most of her time doing mama things. You know - feeding ducks in parks, constructing Halloween costumes, facilitating heated negotiations, reading aloud, throwing raw vegetables on a plate and calling it dinner, and shouting, *"Watch out!"* whenever there are dog piles on the walk to school. Sometimes she writes, but only very occasionally and in the early morning.

*You can find her at:*
**www.MartiDumasBooks.com**

Jaden Toussaint, The Greatest
Episode 1
THE QUEST FOR SCREEN TIME
Written by Marti Dumas
Illustrated by Marie Muravski

# Jaden Toussaint, The Greatest

## The Greatest

Episode 2

# THE LADEK INVASION

# Jaden Toussaint, The Greatest
## The Greatest
### Episode 4
# ATTACK OF THE SWAMP THING

For crafts, recipes, and more, visit:

**www.MartiDumasBooks.com**

Authors love reviews.
We eat them up like
papaya for breakfast.

*Yum!*